Snails can pull up to 200 times their weight.

Some snails have eyes here.

Some here

Snails often take piggyback rides.

pshoo   yawn   strrrrrretch   That was tiring.

SISTER

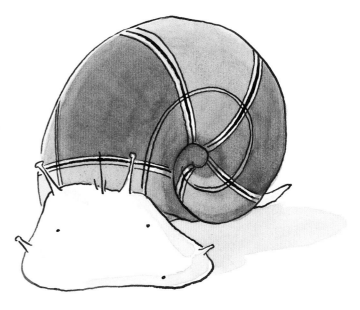

PAPA

snippet

the early riser

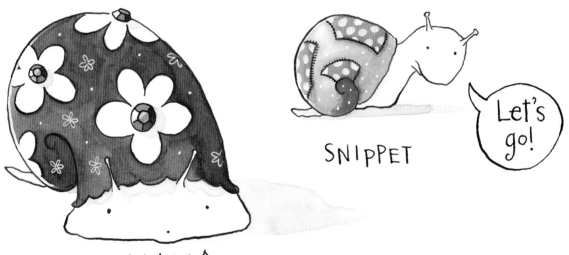

MAMA

SNIPPET

Let's go!

by bethanie deeney murguia

Alfred A. Knopf   New York

With gratitude to my editors, Joanne Taylor and
Michele Burke, for bringing Snippet to life

THIS IS A BORZOI BOOK PUBLISHED BY ALFRED A. KNOPF

Visit us on the Web! randomhouse.com/kids
Educators and librarians, for a variety of teaching tools, visit us at RHTeachersLibrarians.com
Library of Congress Cataloging-in-Publication Data
Murguia, Bethanie Deeney.
Snippet the early riser / Bethanie Deeney Murguia. — 1st ed.
p. cm.
Summary: A little snail who likes to get up early in the morning has trouble waking up his sleepy family.
ISBN 978-1-58246-460-2 (trade) — ISBN 978-1-58246-461-9 (lib. bdg.) — ISBN 978-0-307-98169-1 (ebook)
[1. Snails—Fiction. 2. Family life—Fiction. 3. Sleep—Fiction.] I. Title.
PZ7.M944Sni 2013
[E]—dc23
2012023887

The illustrations in this book were created using watercolor, gouache, and ink.
MANUFACTURED IN MALAYSIA
March 2013   10 9 8 7 6 5 4 3 2 1   First Edition

For the inspiring people and
critters of Spring Street

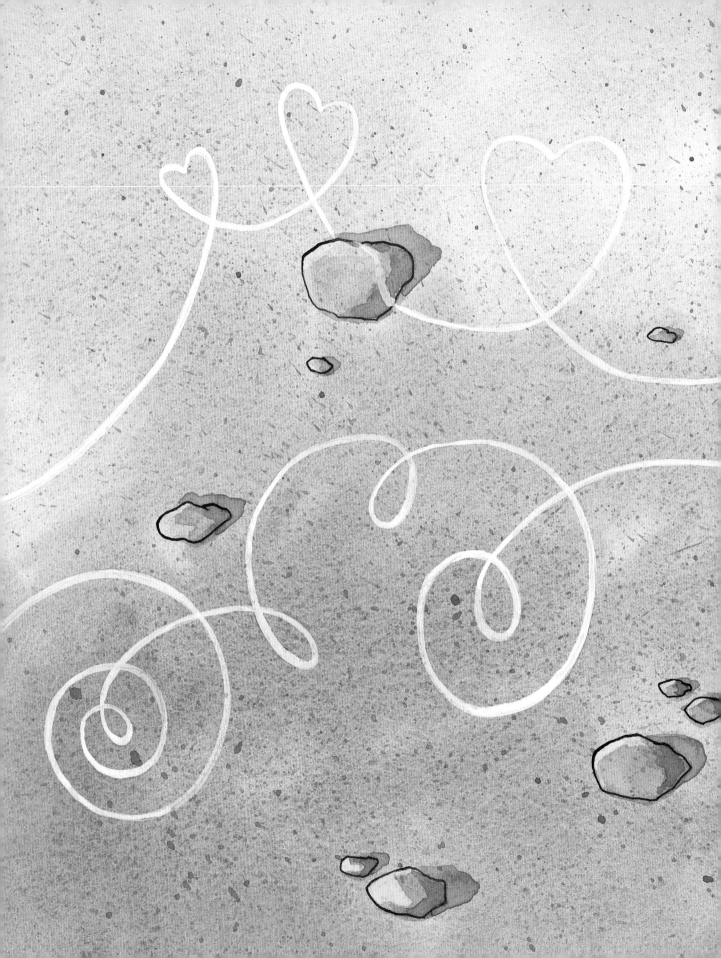

In many ways, Snippet
was an ordinary snail.
He drew on the sidewalk.

I'm dizzy.

He made leaf sculptures.

Don't ruin your appetites.

He played soccer.

He especially adored piggyback rides.

At bedtime, he would
snuggle inside his shell
and fall fast asleep.

Awake

Asleep

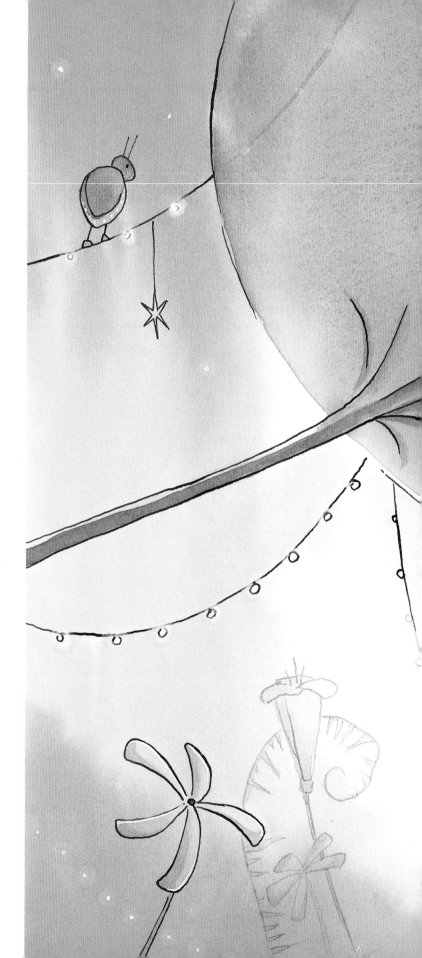

But while his family loved to snooze all morning,
Snippet did not.

At sunrise, long before his family stirred,
Snippet sprang from his shell.

He knocked.

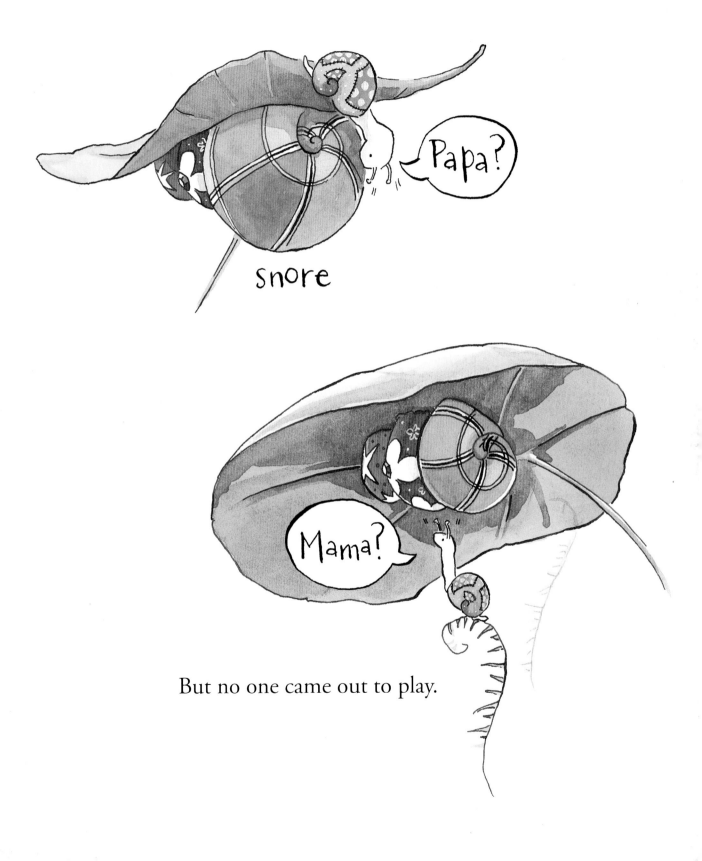

But no one came out to play.

RISE AND SHINE!

Snippet hollered.

He turned on the shower.

Giddyup!

He glided onto Papa's shell for a piggyback ride. Papa yawned. Mama snorted. But no one came out to play.

"Hmph. How did *I* end up with a
family of slugs?" wondered Snippet.

"Let's jump on the bed," said Grasshopper.
"That's *sure* to wake them."

They bounced and bounced.
There was a snore, a wiggle, a twitch.
But still, no one came out to play.

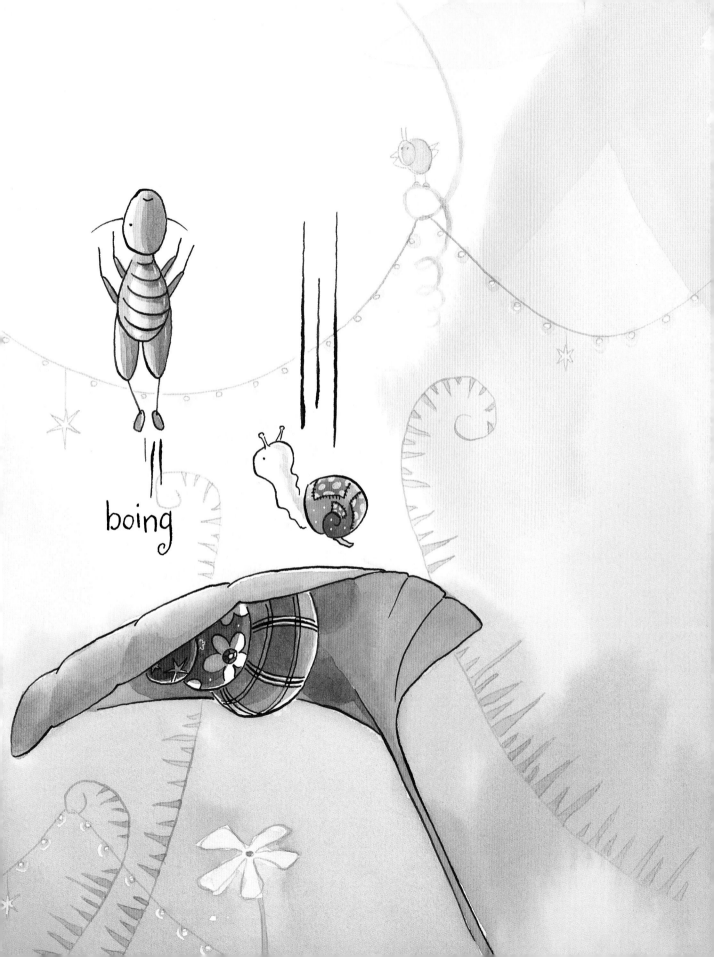

boing

"Let's wake them with music," said Cricket.
Cricket chirped, and Snippet belted out a tune.

"Why don't we push them
out of bed?" suggested Ant.

errgh

They pushed and pushed. Mama wheezed.
Sister snuffled. But still, no one came out to play.

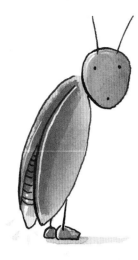

"I could turn on my light,"
said Firefly, wiggling his tail.

"*I* could stink them out,"
offered Stinkbug.

"We'll have none of *that*," declared
Caterpillar. And then he turned
back to his breakfast.

"That's it!" exclaimed Snippet as he watched Caterpillar chewing.

He gathered the family's
favorite leaves.

Then he chomped. And chomped. And chomped.
Until . . .

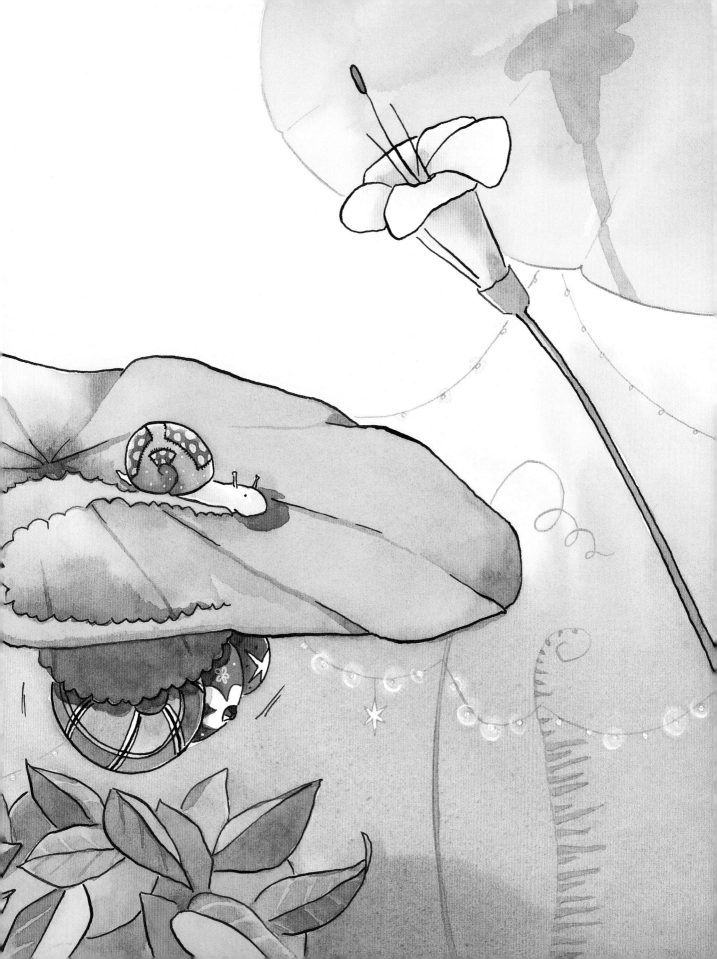

One by one, the snails awoke
to the sweet smell of fresh leaves.

They feasted and feasted.

At last, Snippet's family was ready to play.

"Who wants a piggyback ride?" asked Papa.

"Me, me, me. Let's race to the flowers!" shouted Snippet.
"And then we can draw. And then we'll make sculptures.
And then we'll play soccer."

But before long . . .

Snippet was quiet.

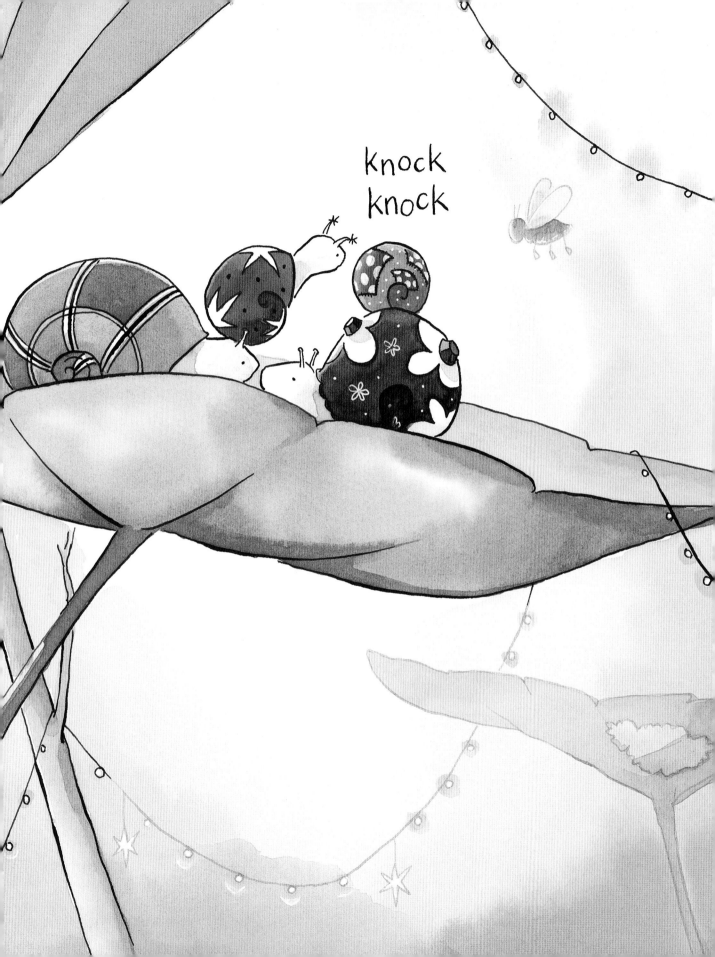

Until the next morning . . .

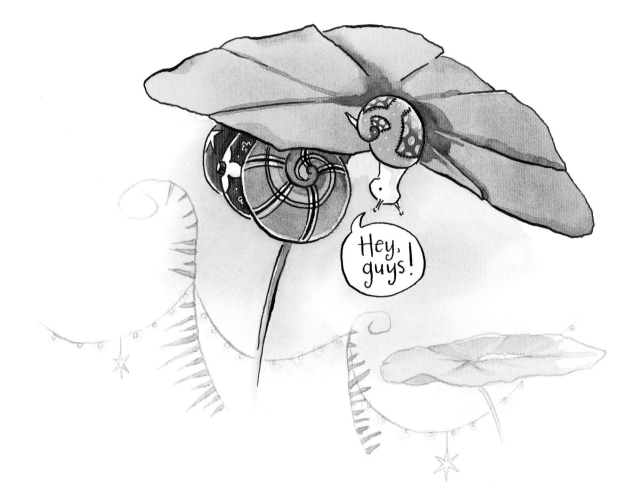

A FEW THINGS YOU SHOULD KNOW ABOUT SNAILS:

Snails sleep a LOT.

Snails wake up very, very slowly.

garumpf   twitch   jiggle   brrr   Zzᶻz